What If?

Just Wondering Poems

What If?

Just Wondering Poems

by Joy N. Hulme

illustrated by Valeri Gorbachev

WORDSONG
BOYDS MILLS PRESS

For those who fill my world with wonder
—J.N.H.

To my children, Konstantin and Sasha
—V.G.

Text copyright © 1993 by Joy N. Hulme
Illustrations copyright © 1993 by Boyds Mills Press
All rights reserved

Published by Wordsong
Boyds Mills Press, Inc.
A Highlights Company
815 Church Street
Honesdale, Pennsylvania 18431
Printed in Singapore

Publisher Cataloging-in-Publication Data
Hulme, Joy N.
    What if ? : just wondering poems / by Joy N. Hulme ; illustrated
by Valeri Gorbachev.
[32] p. : col. ill. ; cm.
Summary : A collection of poems about animals, including "Inchworm," "Gophers," "Termite,"
and "Polliwog."
ISBN 1-56397-186-0
1. Children's poetry—American. 2. Animals—Juvenile poetry.
[1. American poetry. 2. Animals—Poetry.] I. Gorbachev, Valeri, ill.
II. Title.
811.54—dc20   1993
Library of Congress Catalog Card Number 92-60863

First edition, 1993
Book designed by Tim Gillner
The text of this book is set in 14-point Tiffany.
The illustrations are done in pen and ink and watercolors.
Distributed by St. Martin's Press

10 9 8 7 6 5 4 3 2

Contents

HOW COME? AND WHAT IF?

The world is so full of astonishing things:
Spider spun silk, butterfly wings,
Pink petal puffs on an apricot tree,
Spirally shells that sing of the sea,
Quick swishy fishes,
and creatures that crawl,
Enormously big or amazingly small.

With all of these things to delight us about,
There are thousands of questions to wonder about.
How come? And what if?
And suppose this were so?
It's exciting to wonder about what we know.

BUTTERFLY

Did you ever see a butterfly
Flutter by a buttercup
And stop a while
To butter up?

She gets butter on her fingers
While she lingers.

HUMMINGBIRDS

Hummingbirds whir their way about
Backward, forward, in and out.
They have swivel shoulder sockets
And nests so small they'd fit in pockets.
To get a drink, they take a sup
Of nectar from a flower cup;
And for their dinner bill of fare
They snatch some insects from the air.

I wonder if such speedy things
Ever wish to rest their wings.

CRICKET

A cricket sings
By fiddling his wings.

ROLY BUG

See the little roly bug
Curl into a cozy hug.

Does he hide his feet inside
Because he knows
How much he hurts with
Stepped-on toes?

INCHWORM

An inchworm measures wherever he goes.
He humps his back till his tail meets his nose.
He stretches to measure his length and then
He stretches his hump again and again.

GOPHERS

Gophers go for bulbs and roots,
Sweet and tender sprouting shoots.
They always gnaw where they are going,
Everything that's green and growing.

In their dark tunnels underground
How can they see where food is found?

ANTS

The ants play follow-the-leader
Up and over the hills,
Across the walk, around a rock,
And under the daffodils.

What would happen do you think,
If the leader stopped to get a drink?

TERMITE

A termite might bite
On the rafters at night
When he sits down to dine
On fresh sawdusty pine.
Or he may want to munch on
A crunchy chip luncheon.

What a dry and dusty diet!
WOOD you like to try it?

POLLIWOG

Polli, polli, polliwog,
Will you turn into a frog?
Can you come out of disguise,
Grow a pair of bulging eyes,
Turn to green from grayish-grape?
Can you change your swishy shape
To a proper froggy form
Some night when the weather's warm?
Will your tail just melt away
And some legs sprout out one day?
Can a croak grow in your throat?
Will you wear a spotted coat?

Polli, polli, polliwog,
Will you then be Polly Frog?

TOAD

Old toad sits like a lumpy gray stone
Scarcely moving a muscle or bone,
Till quick as a zip
With a lickety flick
Of his stickety tongue
He snatches a snack
And sucks it back.

SQUIRREL

Squirrely with a curly tail
Arching upward like a sail
For balance while you run your races
Over high and wirey places:

Do you hurry and keep busy,
'Cause looking down might
Make you dizzy?

GIRAFFE

I wonder why a giraffe
Can't laugh.

Does gravity pull down so strong
Sound can't climb up a neck that long?

You'd think an animal so tall
Would have the longest laugh of all.

LOBSTER

He's upside down and inside out;
He's backwards and he's sideways.
His bones are out; his skin is in;
He lives in ocean tideways.

He walks on hairy, spindly legs
That smell and breathe and hear,
And scurries backward in retreat
Whenever danger's near.

His jaws chew sideways, but his teeth
Are found inside his tummy;
And while he gobbles fishy fare,
His feet taste if it's yummy.

His kidneys hide inside his head;
His brain's beside his throat;
And when it gets too small for him,
He sheds his bony coat.

He has one claw to clobber with;
The other cuts and saws;
And when he frolics on the beach,
He plays with SANDY CLAWS.

CLAM

A clam clamps shut to hide inside
His smooth and shiny shell.

Without a window in his house
When food swims by, how can he tell?

OCTOPUS

Take my advice and do not fuss
With a sprawling eight-armed octopus.

If he had a hand on every arm
And a glove on every fist,
If you met him in a boxing match,
You'd be more hit than missed.

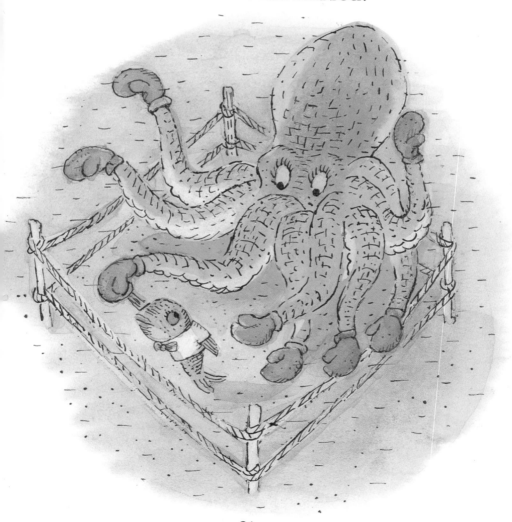

KOALA BEAR

Please don't squeeze a koala bear—
It takes his breath away.
Hold him by the forearms
When you take him out to play.
He lives on eucalyptus leaves
And never needs a drink—

That's bitter bear fare,
Don't you think?

KANGAROO

A kangaroo baby sleeps in a pocket
And keeps his mommy hopping to rock it.

RACCOONS

Do you think that raccoons are afraid of the light?
Why else would they only come out in the night?

Do they coax when they're cozily cuddled to sleep,
"If you'll please leave the dark on, we won't
make a peep"?

FIREFLY

I wonder why the firefly
Glimmers and glows in the evening sky.

Do you suppose he shimmers and shows
To light the way for his lady fly?

ELEPHANT

An elephant's trunk is a useful tool
For squirting water to keep him cool,
For lifting up logs, or testing the trail,
Or holding hands with his mother's tail,
For sucking up peanuts, or hugging up hay,
Or feeding himself in an elephant's way.

But why is it called a TRUNK? Who knows?
It isn't packed for carrying clothes!

BUFFALO

Wouldn't it be fun to know
A shaggly, scraggly buffalo
With bearded chin and hairy hide
And hump-shaped back to climb and ride,
With horns like handles on his head?

You'd best beware of him instead.
'Cause buffalo don't like to play.
Their stony stares say, "Stay away."

BEE

A bee just mostly flies and flits
'Cause his stinger fits
On the place where he sits.

SPIDERS

No wonder spiders wear bare feet
To run their cobweb races.

Suppose they had to have eight shoes.
How would they tie the laces?

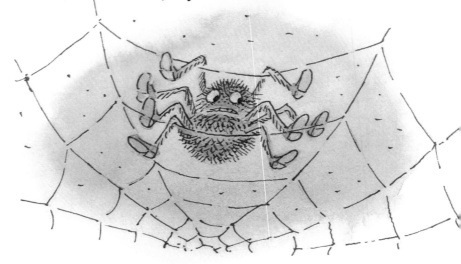

CATERPILLAR

Why does a caterpillar
Wear such a fuzzy coat?

So if a robin swallows him
He'll tickle in his throat.

FLEA

A flea is tiny as can be,
So little you can hardly see.

I wonder how a thing so small
Can cause the BIGGEST itch of all.

LIZARD

If a lizard's suit becomes too small,
He doesn't seem to care at all.
He simply wriggles out of it.
(He wears one underneath to fit.)

With all those layers of clothes on him,
How come a lizard looks so slim?

GRASSHOPPERS

Grasshoppers pop from spot to spot
When the ground is griddle hot.

Think how heavenly it feels
To find a spot to cool their heels.

FLY'S EYES

If you had a million eyes
The same size as a fly's,
Could you read a million
Books at once?

My, but you'd be wise.